THIS BOOK
BELONGS TO:

_____

For Stefan, whose question inspired this book.
—K.H.

For O.K.
—D.T.

www.enchantedlionbooks.com

Text copyright © 2014 by Kirsten Hall
Illustrations copyright © 2014 by Daria Tolstikova

First edition published by Enchanted Lion Books
351 Van Brunt Street, Brooklyn, NY 11231

ISBN 978-1-59270-168-1

First edition 2014

Book layout and production: Tim Palin Creative
Final layout: Sarah Klinger

Printed in China by South China Printing Co. Ltd., Dongguan City, Guangdong Province

10 9 8 7 6 5 4 3 2 1

The Jacket

Words by
Kirsten Hall

Pictures by
Dasha Tolstikova

ENCHANTED LION BOOKS

NEW YORK

Book was a book that had just about everything.

He was solid and strong.
His words were smart and playful.

LET'S GIGGLE!

LOOK!

The problem was, Book didn't feel special.

Day after day, Book longed for a child to discover him.

To disappear into his pages.

To laugh at his story.

To love him and care for him in a way all favorite books know.

Even on days when Book worried he might never be found, he did his best to stand tall.

And all the while, he kept an eye out for the child who would finally notice him.

One day, it happened.

Book fit perfectly into the girl's hands.

She took him everywhere, and Book thought he must be the girl's favorite thing in the whole wide world.

But the truth was that there was someone else whom the girl really loved, too.

EGG CREAM!

Because the girl also loved her dog, Egg Cream.

Book could see why the girl
adored her dog.

He was wild and funny,
furry and sweet.

He scratched at the door.

He rolled around on the floor.

He did neat things with sticks and balls.

He was warm and cozy. And he loved the girl.

For Book, though, Dog was a big problem.

A big, clumsy problem with scary teeth and a huge slippery tongue. He was messy and wet, he licked and drooled.

No, Book didn't like Dog one bit.

Worst of all, Dog was always ruining
Book's perfect moments with the girl.

One especially lovely afternoon, when Book
was resting peacefully in the girl's hands…

Suddenly, there was MUD.
EVERYWHERE!

So much mud that Book could no
longer see a thing! Book was scared,
but did not want to cry. Tears would
ruin his ink and paper.

What had happened?
                              Where was the girl?

Then, Book heard her, an unfamiliar quiver in her voice.

"LOOK what Egg Cream did!" the girl sobbed to her mommy.

"HE BROKE MY BOOK!"

She turned to Egg Cream and shouted:

Henry even told the class all about his
neighbor's pet, Joey.

The day Henry told them

an alien landed in his yard . . .

everyone started asking questions.

Tony said, "You're a big fibber!"

Henry didn't mean to fib . . . it's just that his imagination got mixed up with the truth.

After show and tell, Mr. McCarthy said,
"Henry, you have an amazing imagination.
Instead of using it for show and tell,

why don't you use it to write stories?"

"But . . . what if I can't spell all the words?"
"That's okay—just do your best!" said Mr. McCarthy.
"You can even draw pictures to go with them."